Moritz Petz, alias Udo Weigelt, was born in Hamburg, Germany. Upon completion of his studies, he traveled through Italy, Denmark, and Sweden, working a variety of jobs before returning to study history and German. Today Udo Weigelt lives as a freelance author on Lake Constance.

Amélie Jackowski was born in Toulon, France. She studied at the School of Applied Arts in Strasbourg and at the University of Aix-en-Provence. The illustrator now lives and works in Marseille. She has two children to whom she likes to tell stories she invented.

Moritz Petz | Amélie Jackowski

The Bad Mood!

North
South

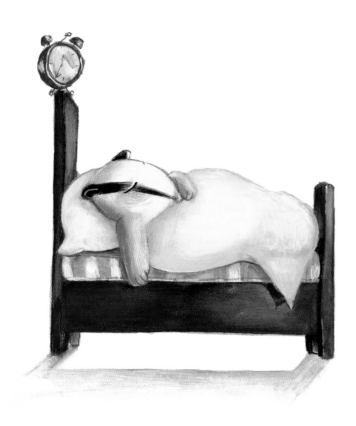

"Humph!" Badger said to himself when he woke up.
"I'm in a bad mood today! This might be dangerous.
Maybe I'd better stay at home."

At breakfast, Badger reconsidered. What was the point of being
in a bad mood if nobody noticed? *Everybody ought to know how
miserable I feel*, he thought. So Badger headed out, slamming the
door behind him.

Badger was going along his usual route when he met Raccoon.
"Good morning, Badger," Raccoon said cheerfully.
"Good morning? What's so good about it?" Badger replied,
and stomped off.
Raccoon was so shocked he didn't say good-bye.

Deer was doing his washing. "Hello there, Badger. Sleep well?"

"None of your business," Badger said.

"Well, excuse me for asking!" said Deer.

Good, thought Badger. *Now Deer and Raccoon know I'm in a bad mood.*

Badger kept going. On his way he met Mouse
and Fox and Hare and Squirrel.
He was as rude to them as he could be.

When he was finished with his morning walk, Badger came back home and started to work in his garden.
As he was digging and weeding, the strangest thing happened. His bad mood just slipped right off him as if it had been a shirt that was too hot to wear. Badger became so happy that he started to whistle a sweet song.

Badger didn't stop working until late that afternoon.
He was deeply satisfied with himself. He went out to the clearing to
play with the other animals. But the woods were still and silent. Not
an animal appeared.

Strange, thought Badger. *Where are they all?*
He went to Raccoon's house to ask.
Raccoon was not in a good mood. "Leave me alone!" he grumbled.
Badger was shocked. No one had ever been so rude to him before.

It wasn't any better with the other animals.
Fox told him to get lost.
Squirrel hurled a nut at his head.
Mouse and Hare shouted and hissed at Badger,
which made him quite dizzy.

Badger was miserable. When Crow came to visit, he told her about how mean all the animals had been to him.

"There must be a reason," said Crow.

Badger thought about it. "Well," he said finally. "I was in a bad mood this morning, and I guess I took it out on my friends. I was very rude to them." Badger felt just awful. "Oh, dear! What can I do?"

Crow and Badger thought about the problem together.

Suddenly Badger jumped up. "I have an idea!" he said. "Will you help me?"

"Indeed I will," said Crow.

"Party tonight!" cawed Crow as she fluttered through the forest.
"Everyone who is in a bad mood is invited! Come to the clearing at
moonrise for a bad-mood party!"
And since Badger had passed his bad mood on to the other animals,
they all showed up at the party. When they saw Badger standing in
the clearing, they glared angrily at him.

Badger took a deep breath. "I want to apologize," he said.
"This morning, I was in an awful mood, and I took it out on all of you.
You are my friends, and it was a terrible thing for me to do. I am so
sorry. Will you please forgive me?"
At last the animals smiled.
Together they sang songs and danced until dawn.